LION AND MOUSE

CATALINA ECHEVERRI

JONATHAN CAPE | LONDON

Once upon a time, a mighty lion and
a tiny mouse lived next to each other.

Although they were different . . .

But there was one problem . . .

. . . Lion thought he was much better
than Mouse in every way.

And he said so.

All day, every day.

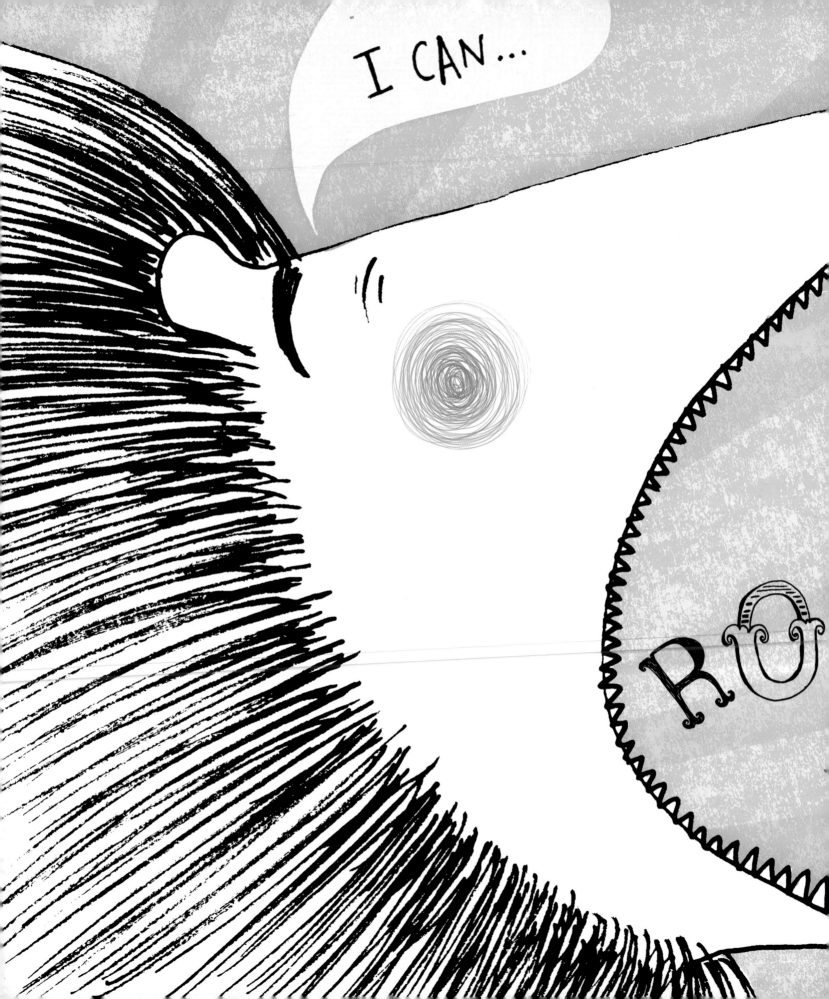

It just never stopped.

So much so that Lion didn't even notice
when his friend Mouse wasn't there any more.

In fact that wasn't true.
Lion was terrified of . . .

. . . the dark!

Mouse heard Lion calling for
him. But would he want to
help his boastful friend?

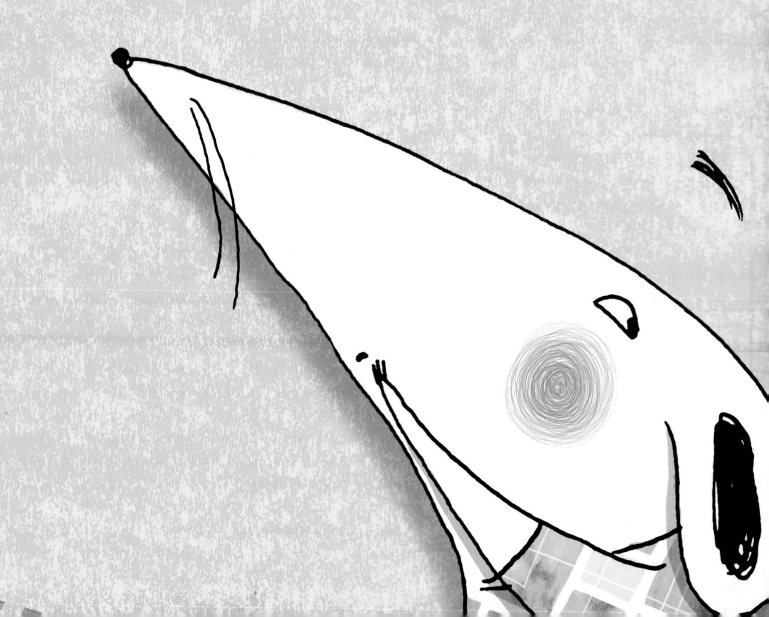

I WANT MOUSE, BUT HE ISN'T HERE. I'M SO SORRY, MOUSE– WHEREVER YOU ARE!

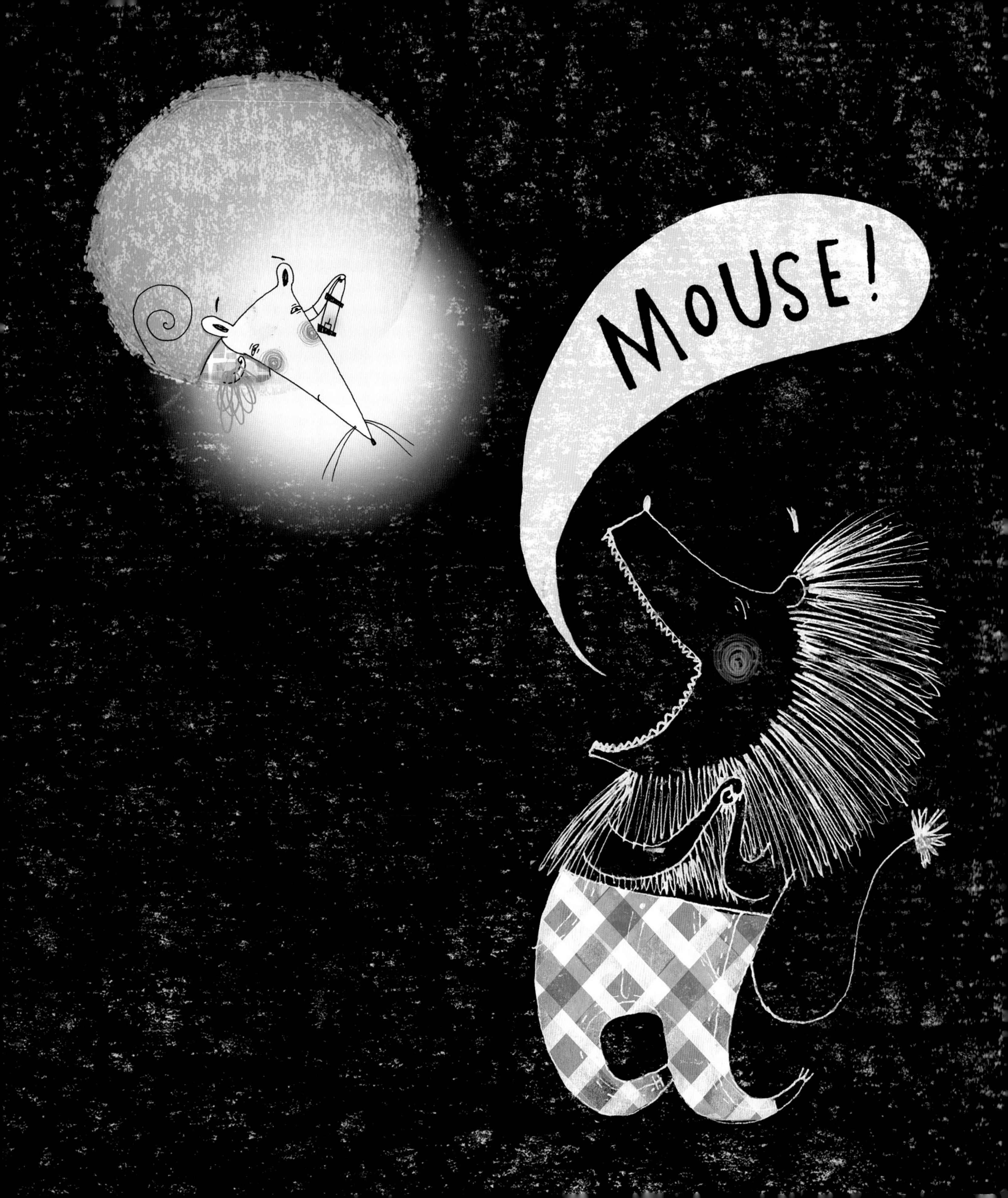
MOUSE!

Lion thanked brave
little Mouse for saving him.
Now he knew what
true friends were for . . .

 . . . helping,

 sharing,

and having lots
of fun together.

From that day on, Lion and Mouse were the best . . .

To my dear parents, friends and tutors,
but most of all to my loving God.

LION AND MOUSE
A JONATHAN CAPE BOOK 978 1 780 08017 8

Published in Great Britain by Jonathan Cape, an imprint of Random House Children's Publishers UK
A Random House Group Company

This edition published 2013

1 2 3 4 5 6 7 8 9 10

RANDOM HOUSE CHILDREN'S PUBLISHERS UK
61–63 Uxbridge Road, London W5 5SA

www.randomhousechildrens.co.uk
www.randomhouse.co.uk

Addresses for companies within The Random House Group Limited
can be found at: www.randomhouse.co.uk/offices.htm

THE RANDOM HOUSE GROUP Limited Reg. No. 954009

A CIP catalogue record for this book is available from the British Library.

Printed in China